THE POST OFFICE CAT

written and illustrated by

GAIL E. HALEY

Methuen Children's Books

London

This edition first published 1979
by Methuen Children's Books Ltd,
11 New Fetter Lane, London E C 4 P 4 E E
First published in Great Britain 1976
by The Bodley Head Ltd,
9 Bow Street, London W C 2 E 7 A L
Copyright © 1976 Gail E. Haley
Printed in Great Britain by
William Clowes & Sons Ltd, Beccles
Separations by Colourcraftsmen Ltd, Chelmsford
ISBN 0 416 87420 7

This book is dedicated to the memory of gentle Starbright-Black-Paws and to Amelia Birdheart; with thanks to Marguerite and Geoffrey for changing the sandbox; to Arnold for putting up with our Catomania; to Clarence for posing; and the many kittens, cats and cat people who contributed. Grateful acknowledgement to the archivists of Bruce Castle Museum, The Victoria and Albert Museum, and the Post Office Historical Records.

Too many cats lived on the dairy farm. There were cats in the barn, cats in the sheds, cats in the hayloft, and a grandfather puss who lived in the farmhouse. Twice a day, after milking, a pan of milk was set out for them; but there was never enough to go round.

When he was almost grown, Clarence, the most adventurous young cat, felt a need for a place of his own, so he stowed away on a milk wagon bound for the city. He dozed during the long, bumpy journey. When they reached the crest of a hill, he sat up quivering with excitement. Below them spread houses, churches, turrets, chimneys, and the spires of London golden in the early morning sun.

The wagon stopped to unload the milk; Clarence jumped down and set off to explore. He found his way into a beautiful park. There were flower gardens, trees to climb, and pools containing tempting goldfish. Friendly people glided along the paths, or sat on the grass sunning themselves and having picnics. Clarence wandered among them, was petted, and fed choice left overs.

A hokey-pokey wagon came down the path, ringing its bell. Children left their parents and clustered round the vendor, clamouring to buy his ice-cream. Clarence, his eyes closed with pleasure, lapped up whatever ice-cream puddles he found. Then, purring, he fell asleep on a park bench.

Clarence lived in the park all through the summer, finding plenty of food, and feeling pleased with himself for having left the dairy farm.

Then quite suddenly it was autumn. The leaves fell from the trees, and the wind grew cold. Workmen boarded up the gazebos and bandstands. The hokey-pokey wagon came no more; the park was deserted. Clarence was without food or shelter. His cat instincts told him it was time to look for a home.

The noisy streets and squares of the city frightened him. It was too dangerous to cross from one side to the other. Omnibuses, carriages and hansom cabs clopped smartly along the cobblestones. Busy people rushed here and there on the pavements; they were all in a hurry. No one noticed Clarence, or seemed to care that he was alone.

Clarence wandered beside a canal. The brightly-painted barges looked inviting, but fierce watchdogs guarded their decks. They made it clear that there was no room aboard for him.

Clarence made his way to Billingsgate, where the fishing boats docked. Porters rushed from the docks with baskets of eels, squid, and oysters. Crabs, lobsters, and fish of all kinds and sizes were stacked in boxes and crates. A kindly-looking man in apron and gaiters stooped to put down a basket. Clarence looked up at him hungrily.

"Blow me down, look who's applying for a job," he shouted to his mates. "Go on, scat! We don't need any more fish tasters 'round 'ere." He threw a small fish to the cat. Gratefully, Clarence dragged it behind a crate and ate it.

Clarence preferred the quieter parts of the city. He spent many days walking along the narrow, shop-lined streets. The smells of sausages, cheeses, spices, and freshly baked bread wafted from the doors.

Through the windows of the cook shop, Clarence saw piles of baked potatoes, and chops sizzling over the grill. He was cold and wished a shopkeeper would take him in.

But each shop window already had its cat. Snug, secure working cats lay curled against the glass, sleeping contentedly. At the end of the day, when the shutters were drawn, they would get up, stretch, and yawn.

Then those lucky cats prowled around their shops, catching mice and guarding their territory. Clarence's once proud tail now drooped sadly behind him.

Clarence found himself on a very grand street. All the houses were surrounded by high walls. The gate to one was ajar, and he slunk through it into the garden. Birds fluttered round a birdbath, pecking at seeds and crumbs that had been put out for them. Clarence looked hopefully towards the house, wondering if there might be room inside for him.

Footsore and tired, he fell asleep on the kitchen step. A little girl who lived there found him and took him in. She fed him left overs and a saucer of milk. Clarence slept that night by the embers on the kitchen hearth. In the morning, the cook found him there, and shooed him out of the door with a broom.

"Away with you. The missus don't like cats."

One freezing midwinter night Clarence discovered the rubbish barrels outside Smithfield Market. He nosed around them cautiously until he found a bone on which there was still a sliver of meat.

No sooner had he picked it up, than he was surrounded by a pack of fierce alley cats. Wherever he looked, he saw the gleam of their eyes. The leader advanced on his belly hissing, "Push off, country cat. This is our haunt. There's no room for anyone else."

The others yowled and snarled their agreement. Clarence's fur stood on end. He arched his back in order to look as large as possible, and sidled away stiff-legged until he was out of reach of their claws. Then he turned and ran through the night as fast as he could.

Clarence sought safety by climbing a tree, and from there he jumped onto a roof. He leaped from one rooftop to the next until he found a sheltered nook warmed by chimney pots. He licked his fur, curled up with his nose buried in his tail, and dreamed of his gentle mother and his warm brothers and sisters. As he slept, the night grew bitterly cold, and heavy clouds formed over London.

In the morning, Clarence looked out over the rooftops. He saw a sleepy sparrow, and stalked it over the tiles. But it flew away when he pounced. Snowflakes began falling from the dark winter sky. Clarence slid down a drain-pipe. He tried to find the street where the dairy wagon delivered the milk. He was tired, discouraged, and hungry, and longed to go home, back to the dairy farm.

It snowed all that day. Yellow lights gleamed from the windows, but the streets were empty. No one wanted to be out in such miserable weather. Suddenly Clarence smelled food. He followed his nose down a derelict alley, and came upon a group of street people seeking shelter in doorways. A ragged old man stirred a bubbling pot over a flaming brazier. Clarence crouched in the fire's warmth. The old man smiled at him.

"Hungry are you, mate? You can share what we have."

When the others gathered round to eat their meal, a small portion was put down for Clarence. After they had all eaten, a thin little girl shyly stroked his head. He rubbed against her leg. Soon he was purring in her lap as she huddled against her parents for warmth. Both girl and cat fell asleep and did not wake until the grey morning.

The snow had finally stopped, but it lay thick on the ground. The street people gathered their meagre belongings and dispersed. The little girl turned to watch Clarence as her parents led her away. Then Clarence set off on his own once more, leaving paw prints in the snow.

He was attracted by the sound of voices, and followed a wagon to the back of a large impressive building. Fascinated, he sat down to watch the employees of Her Majesty's Post Office unloading and carrying in the bags of mail. The door was open, so Clarence walked inside. No one noticed him.

Walking through the sorting room, he reached the front office. There he found a terrible commotion—a crowd of angry, shouting people. Clarence crept forward to see what was happening.

The postmaster stood on a stool trying to keep order. A gentleman waved a mouse-chewed envelope; an important message had been destroyed as it lay in the sorting bins. A governess held up a box of biscuits, gnawed before it arrived in the post. One of the night cleaning ladies threatened to leave because a rat had fallen on her as she was sweeping beneath the stairs. Clerks complained that rats and mice had gnawed rubbers, walked on ink pads, and made nests in the stamp drawers. The mail sorters grumbled that their steak-and-kidney pies were eaten before they could get to their lunch parcels.

A pile of mail had been poured at the postmaster's feet, the addresses so chewed that they could not be delivered. On top of this mutilated heap sat a cheeky mouse, calmly nibbling the corner of an envelope. Others scurried over everything. The distraught postmaster shouted over the uproar, "What we need is a CAT!"

As if on command, Clarence leapt into the middle of the pile in one bound. He caught the offending mouse, and looked up at the postmaster expectantly, swishing his tail. The postmaster patted him on the head, and hired him on the spot. That afternoon, the postmaster sent a petition to his superior, asking that a salary be paid to his Post Office Cat.

Clarence soon rid the Post Office of rats and mice. Mail was delivered unchewed. Stamps and lunches remained intact. Clarence was granted a permanent home, sixpence a week for milk, and all the mice he could catch.

He was a favourite with grateful clerks who petted him, talked to him, and fed him treats. They even had a special collar made for him from which hung a medal. On it was engraved: H.M.P.O.C.— Her Majesty's Post Office Cat. Every evening, after clerks and sorters went home, and the cleaning women finished sweeping, Clarence would wake, stretch, yawn, and prowl from one end of the Post Office to the other. He was happy. He had a place of his own at last.

HISTORICAL NOTE

During the 1800's London was overrun by mice and rats. They lived in sewers, alleys, attics, and pantries. They infested the waterfront and tunnelled under buildings. Pedlars sold hand-carved rat traps and poisons in the streets. Private homes and public buildings kept cats or hired professional rat killers. Jack Black, Rat Catcher by appointment to Her Majesty Queen Victoria, wore a special uniform, and a belt emblazoned with VR (Victoria Regina) flanked by two pewter rats.

In 1868, an official of Her Majesty's Post Office reported widespread mouse mutilation of the mails and money orders. "Traps and other means have to no purpose been used for the riddance of these vermin, and I beg to state that I have requested the resident porter, Tye, to procure three cats for the purpose . . . I understand that a penny-ha'penny is usually allowed at the museums and other places of the kind for each cat kept."

Nine months later he reported, "It is certain that the cat system has answered exceedingly well, and that the cats have done their duty very efficiently."

Post Offices were henceforth authorized to put cats on their payrolls. Postmasters were required to furnish periodic "cat efficiency reports" which are on file today at London's main Post Office.

In 1953, questions were asked in Parliament as to whether the cats' pay scale had kept pace with the times, and whether female felines were given equal opportunities and maternity benefits. The Right Honourable Mr L. D. Gammons, M.P., Assistant Post-master General, reassured the Members on all these points.

To this day, cats continue to be employed in Post Offices throughout Great Britain.